First US edition 2020
First published by Templar Books, an imprint of Bonnier Books UK 2020

Library of Congress Catalog Card Number pending
ISBN 978-1-5362-1556-4 (hardcover)
ISBN 978-1-5362-1665-3 (paperback)

20 21 22 23 24 25 TLF 10 9 8 7 6 5 4 3 2 1

Printed in Dongguan, Guangdong, China

This book was typeset in Kosmik BoldOne and Kosmik PlainTwo.
The illustrations were created digitally.

Candlewick Entertainment
an imprint of
Candlewick Press
99 Dover Street
Somerville, Massachusetts 02144

www.candlewick.com

GIGANTOSAURUS™

THE GROUNDWOBBLER

CANDLEWICK
ENTERTAINMENT

The little dinosaurs were playing at one of their
favorite places, the hot spring next to the volcano.

Bill was hanging out by a mud pool while Mazu and Tiny watched
the geysers shoot water up into the air.

But instead of relaxing, Rocky was having fun jumping INTO a geyser. As it erupted, it blasted him high above the treetops—knocking Archie out of his tree!

Poor Archie flapped his wings frantically, but he wasn't very good at flying.

Archie fell with a CRASH and a SPLASH into a mud pool. The sound startled Bill. Was that Gigantosaurus coming for his bath?

"Don't worry, it's just Archie," said Tiny, chuckling.

"I can stay on the lookout for Giganto!" said Archie. "But first I need to get back in my tree. . . ."

Mazu knew just what to do. She led Archie to a geyser and stirred up the bubbles with her tail. WHOOSH! A jet of water blasted Archie back into the treetops.

Woo-hoo!
I'm FLYING!

Suddenly the ground began to shake, making Bill even MORE nervous.
"It's just the volcano rumbling, Bill," said Mazu kindly, getting a snack out
of her bag. She knew that food always made Bill feel better.

But the rumbling got louder and louder. Mazu was wrong.
This wasn't the volcano. It was a GROUNDWOBBLER!

"Everyone hold on to me!" shouted Rocky, taking the lead.

Mazu reached out for Rocky's shoulders and Tiny followed behind. Bill brought up the rear, looking around anxiously. Together they marched away from the volcano toward home, singing a song as they went.

WOBBLE, WOBBLE, WOB-BLE! WOBBLE, WOBBLE, WOB-BLE!

Before they had gone far, the ground in front of them split open with a loud CRACK. Mazu pulled Rocky back from the edge just in time, but now the four dinos were stuck.

In front of them was a gaping crevice!

"The wobble's over, Bill! Why are you still shaking?" Tiny asked.

"I'm s-s-scared!" said Bill. "How are we going to get back to the den?"

"Let's jump across!" suggested Rocky.

JUMP? That's COCONUTS!

Mazu spotted a vine on a palm tree at the edge of the crevice. It would make the perfect rope swing to get them across the gap.

"I have a very bad feeling about this," groaned Bill.

Rocky went first. He grabbed hold of the vine, took a running start, swung up into the air . . .

I'm a super para-lalla . . . para-something-or-other!

and landed on the other side of the crevice.
Archie walked by just at the wrong moment.
"Hi everyone! Where's Rocky?" he asked—seconds before
the dino landed right on top of him!

Found him!

Rocky looked at Archie and grinned.
"At least we know the swing works!"

The vine swung back to Mazu. "Do you want to go next, Bill?" she asked.

Bill shook his head. "I'm going to stay right here where it's safe," he said.

But it WASN'T safe. From nearby, they heard a mighty ROAR. Mazu, Bill, and Tiny were on the same side of the crevice as GIGANTO! The only way to escape was over the gap.

Bill quickly changed his mind about the swing. He grabbed the vine and leapt into the air, but instead of flying across, he was left dangling in the crevice.

Tiny came to the rescue. Using her triceratops strength, she grabbed the other end of the vine and pulled Bill out.

Bill was very glad to be back on solid ground, but the friends still needed to find a way across. Luckily, Giganto seemed to have lost interest in the little dinos and had stomped toward the geysers.

Mazu spotted Archie on the other side and another idea sprang to mind. "That's it!" she gasped. "We can FLY over!"

Tiny wasn't so sure. Archie HADN'T flown—he had been blasted over by a geyser!

A minute later, Bill looked up to see Mazu sitting proudly on top of a homemade catapult. She had secured the vine from the tree under a rock, pulling the tree way back, and once the rock was pushed aside, Mazu would be flung across the gap.

Presenting the Dino Launcher 3000!

Mazu was ready for liftoff. Tiny pushed the rock away and—PINNNGG!—the tree was released, flinging the little ankylosaurus into the air.

And we have a perfect launch!

She sailed over the crevice, and just like Rocky she had a nice soft landing—right on top of Archie!

Archie rubbed his head. "How do I manage to crash when I'm not the one flying?"

Mazu got to her feet. Now only Tiny and Bill were left to cross.

Tiny took Bill's hand. It was OK to be scared, she told him. They were ALL scared!

"As long as I have my friends around to help me, I know I'll be all right," she said.
"How about we go together?"

Bill beamed at her. That made him feel much better.

Bill climbed onto the Dino Launcher 3000 while Tiny hurried around to move the rock. Archie, Mazu, and Rocky watched nervously from the other side.

"WATCH OUT!" shouted Archie from his tree. He, Mazu, and Rocky had spotted . . .

GIGANTOSAURUS!

Giganto stomped toward the Dino Launcher 3000 and bent down to take a look. His huge tail swung toward Tiny and pinned her to the rock. She was stuck!

"Bill!" Tiny called. "If you cut the vine, you can escape! I'll find a way across later."

Bill was still afraid, but there was no way he was leaving his friend behind.

He caught sight of the hot spring and had a brilliant idea.
It was time for Bill to be brave.

"Hey, Giganto!" he shouted, jumping into a geyser.

Bill stirred up the bubbles just like Mazu had done earlier. Sure enough,
a jet of water erupted into the air. Forgetting about the little dinos,
Giganto stepped into the spring to enjoy a hot shower.

Bill rushed back to the Dino Launcher 3000, and together he and Tiny climbed up onto it. Tiny tried to cut the vine to release the trunk, but it was too tough!

They heard a single loud STOMP and looked up to see GIGANTO! The little dinos cowered as he loomed over them—but then he sniffed the air and turned away.

"Is he going to leave us alone?" Bill said hopefully.

As Giganto walked away, his tail knocked the rock off the vine. The Dino Launcher 3000 was finally released, and Bill and Tiny glided through the air.

We're flying!

Here we come!

Now it was their turn to crash-land on top of unlucky Archie!

"You were really brave, Bill," Tiny said as she leapt to her feet. "I'm so proud of you!"

"I was so worried about you, I forgot to be worried about myself," Bill said. "And you know what? Flying felt great!"

Now Bill knew that when his friends were around, there was no need to be afraid.

Back at home, everyone was talking about Bill's great adventure.

"You should have seen Bill stir up that geyser right in front of Giganto," said Rocky. "He was so brave!"

"We learned something new about Giganto, too," said Mazu. "He likes to take showers in the geysers!"

Bill decided to try a geyser shower, too. But when he jumped in—WHOOSH!—the jet of water was higher than he expected.

"Geysers aren't fun at all!" Bill wailed. "Someone get me down!"

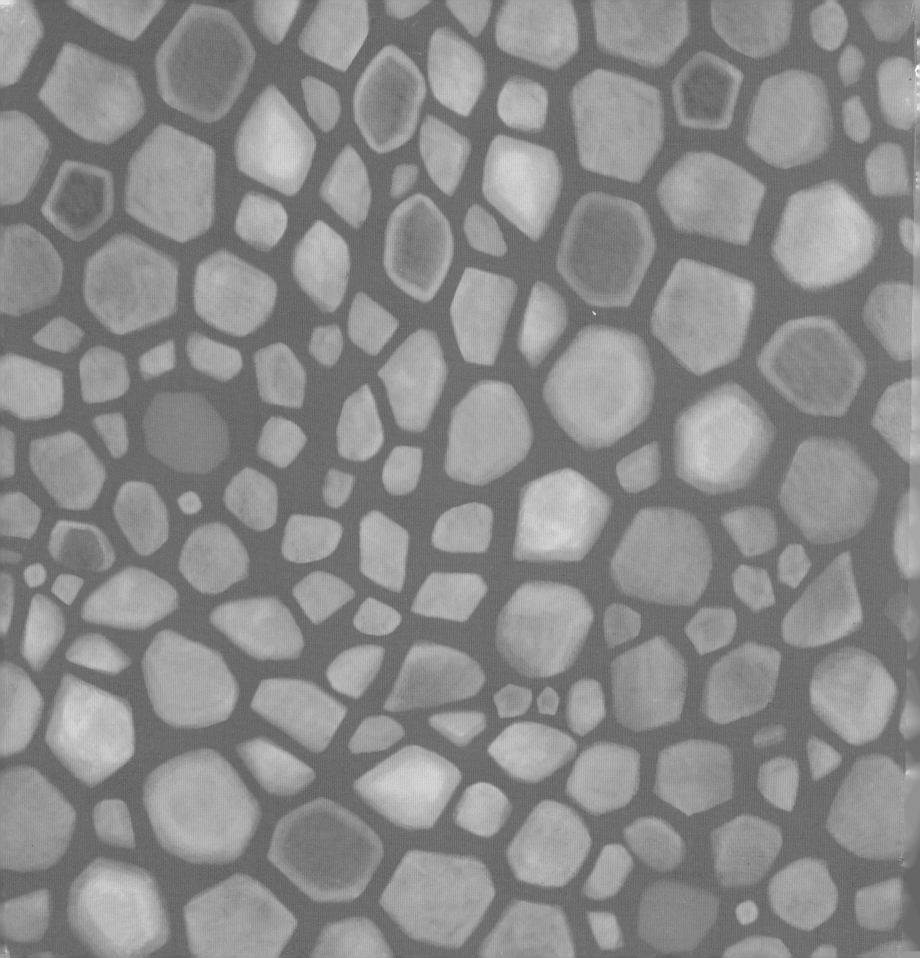